First published 1989 by Walker Books Ltd
87 Vauxhall Walk, London SE11 5HJ

Text © 1989 Anne Carter
Illustrations © 1989 Anne Dalton

First printed 1989
Printed in Hong Kong by South China Printing Co.

British Library Cataloguing in Publication Data
Carter, Anne
The twelve dancing princesses.
I. Title   II. Dalton, Anne
823'.914[J]

ISBN 0-7445-1115-1

THE TWELVE DANCING PRINCESSES

Retold by Anne Carter
Illustrated by Anne Dalton

WALKER BOOKS
LONDON

Once upon a time there was a boy whose work it was to mind the cattle for a farmer. He had lost his father and mother and was all alone in the world, although his blue eyes and happy smile won him many friends and the village girls looked kindly on him. But the boy, whose name was Michael, did not notice them, for his eyes were full of stars and his head was full of dreams. In those dreams he stood in a kingly hall surrounded by a dozen beautiful princesses, one of whom he might choose to be his bride.

One hot summer's day, when Michael was just eighteen years old, he ate his lunch of bread and cheese as usual and lay down under a hawthorn bush, shielding his eyes against the sun.

As he lay half-waking, dreaming his customary dream, there appeared to him a lady, very tall and beautiful, dressed in a robe of cloth of gold, who said, "Michael, leave your cattle and go to the Castle Belvedere and there you shall marry a princess."

All that afternoon Michael thought about the lady's words but by the evening he had decided they must have been only a part of his dream and put them out of his mind.

The next day, as he dozed beneath the hawthorn, she appeared again, with the self-same words, "Michael, go to the Castle Belvedere and you shall marry a princess."

That evening, as the young men and girls idled round the well in the village square, Michael told them about the lady and her words but they only laughed at him and called him a dreamer.

But on the third day the same thing happened again and this time Michael, who was growing bored with minding cattle, began to think that no harm could come from doing as he was told.

With that he drove his cattle home, even though it was only two o'clock in the afternoon, collected his wages from the farmer and, with his few belongings tied up in a bundle on his shoulder, set off to seek his fortune.

He walked for many days, earning his food and lodging when he could by such jobs as sawing wood, mending pots (for he was nimble with his fingers) or minding children, and asking always where he might find the Castle Belvedere. But it was not until he had been travelling for nearly a year and left the countryside he knew far, far behind him, that he heard anything of the place he sought. By this time his clothes were travel-worn and shabby and his blue eyes a deal less innocent than when he set out, for he had had many desperate adventures on the way.

He had been given a lodging for the night at a small ale house whose landlord was grateful for a few hours digging in his vegetable garden and after supper, as he sat by the fire in the tap room, Michael asked as usual if anyone present could tell him the whereabouts of the Castle Belvedere. To his surprise, instead of the head-shakings he was accustomed to, he saw broad grins spread over the faces of all the company.

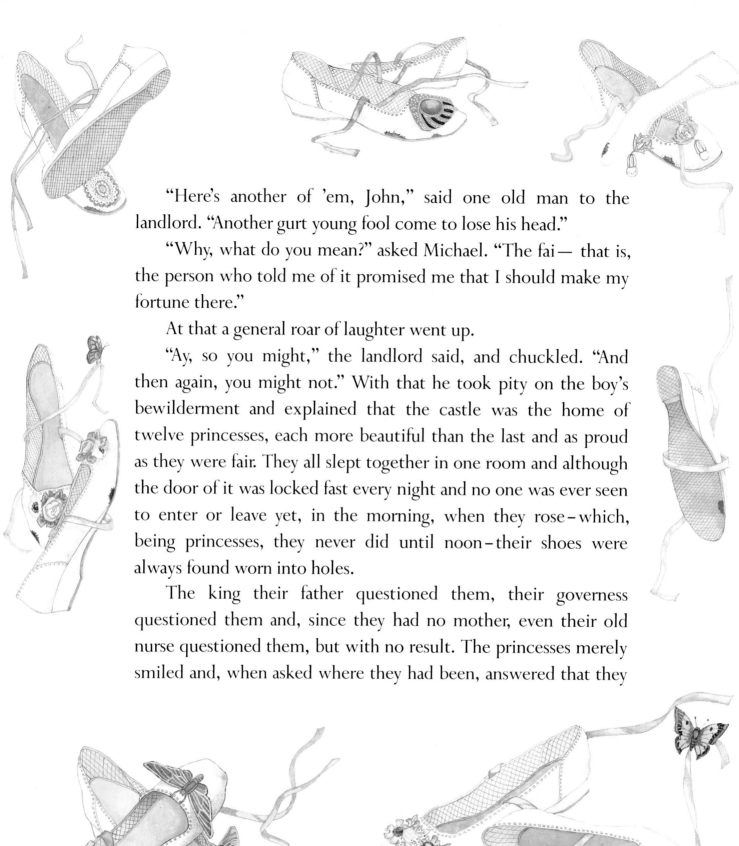

"Here's another of 'em, John," said one old man to the landlord. "Another gurt young fool come to lose his head."

"Why, what do you mean?" asked Michael. "The fai— that is, the person who told me of it promised me that I should make my fortune there."

At that a general roar of laughter went up.

"Ay, so you might," the landlord said, and chuckled. "And then again, you might not." With that he took pity on the boy's bewilderment and explained that the castle was the home of twelve princesses, each more beautiful than the last and as proud as they were fair. They all slept together in one room and although the door of it was locked fast every night and no one was ever seen to enter or leave yet, in the morning, when they rose – which, being princesses, they never did until noon – their shoes were always found worn into holes.

The king their father questioned them, their governess questioned them and, since they had no mother, even their old nurse questioned them, but with no result. The princesses merely smiled and, when asked where they had been, answered that they

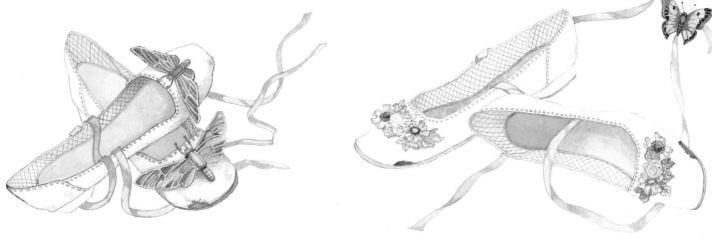

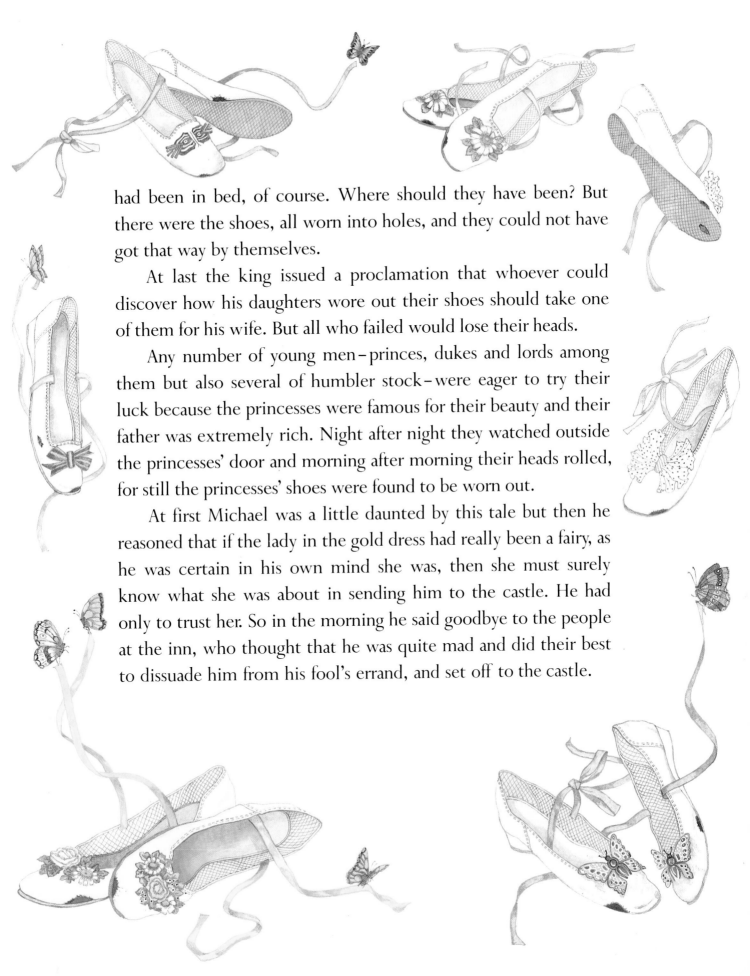

had been in bed, of course. Where should they have been? But there were the shoes, all worn into holes, and they could not have got that way by themselves.

At last the king issued a proclamation that whoever could discover how his daughters wore out their shoes should take one of them for his wife. But all who failed would lose their heads.

Any number of young men – princes, dukes and lords among them but also several of humbler stock – were eager to try their luck because the princesses were famous for their beauty and their father was extremely rich. Night after night they watched outside the princesses' door and morning after morning their heads rolled, for still the princesses' shoes were found to be worn out.

At first Michael was a little daunted by this tale but then he reasoned that if the lady in the gold dress had really been a fairy, as he was certain in his own mind she was, then she must surely know what she was about in sending him to the castle. He had only to trust her. So in the morning he said goodbye to the people at the inn, who thought that he was quite mad and did their best to dissuade him from his fool's errand, and set off to the castle.

When he came there, he did not present himself immediately as one who would try to find out the princesses' secret. Instead he went round to the head gardener and asked to be taken on. As luck would have it, there was a vacancy and Michael found himself set to assist the man responsible for the cut flowers for the palace.

His chief duty was to wait each day at noon, with twelve bouquets of flowers, ready to present one to each of the princesses as they emerged from their room.

On the first day, he took up his stand outside the door, carrying his basket. The princesses floated out, chattering merrily to one another but, as they took the flowers, not one deigned to give so much as a look to the boy who held them. Not one, that is, until the last. The youngest princess, whose name was Lina, gazed at him with eyes as dark and soft as velvet and exclaimed, "Oh! We have a new garden boy! How pretty he is!"

One or two of the princesses tittered, but the eldest told her severely that princesses ought not to notice such things.

Michael, for his part, had looked hard at all the princesses as they passed him. Most of them he thought proud, disagreeable girls, and not half as pretty as the shepherdesses in his village at home, but that one look from the lovely Princess Lina made him determined to try his fate.

That night, the lady in the gold dress came to him again. This time she brought with her two small laurel trees, a rose laurel and a cherry laurel. She also gave him a small golden rake, a golden watering-can and a silken towel.

"Michael," she said to him, "plant these two laurels in two tubs, rake them, water them and wipe their leaves with this silken towel. When they are grown as tall as a girl of fifteen, say to each, 'My beautiful laurel, with this golden rake I have raked you, with this golden can I have watered you, with this silken towel I have wiped you.' Then ask for anything you choose and the laurel will grant it you."

With that, the lady vanished, almost before he could thank her. And there were the trees, the rake, the towel and the watering-can to prove to him that it was not a dream.

The plants grew very fast. When they were as tall as a girl of fifteen, Michael said to the cherry laurel,

"My beautiful laurel, with this golden rake I have raked you, with this golden can I have watered you, with this silken towel I have wiped you. Grant me now the power to become invisible."

At once a sprig of small white flowers appeared on the tree. He plucked it, stuck it in his buttonhole and was instantly invisible.

When night fell and the princesses went up to bed, who should creep after them but Michael. He followed them into their room, hid himself under Princess Lina's bed and heard the door locked upon them. As soon as the palace was quiet and everyone asleep, up jumped all the twelve princesses, whispering and giggling excitedly. Running to their closets they pulled out their exquisite ball gowns and dressed their powdered hair high on their heads. Jewels glimmered at their throats and wrists and on the toes of their brand new satin shoes.

When all were ready, the eldest sister clapped her hands and instantly a doorway opened in the wall. One by one the princesses bent their heads and entered. Last of all came Michael. He followed them down a wide stone stair but, half-way down, he trod on the train of Princess Lina, who was last.

She cried out, "Oh! There is someone behind me snatching at my dress!"

"Don't be so foolish," called back her eldest sister. "Who could be there? You must have caught it on a nail."

Down and down they went until they came to a passage ending in a wooden door. The princesses went through it, into a beautiful wood where the trees were all of silver and shone like water in the cold moonlight.

From there they passed into a second wood where the trees were of gleaming gold, and then into a third where every leaf and twig sparkled with diamonds.

The third wood ended on the shore of a broad lake. On the far side of it was a castle. Music floated over the water. Drawn up below the bank were twelve little boats, each with a lantern in the stern and a handsome prince waiting to pole it across. They handed the princesses into the boats and Michael stepped neatly into the last, which held the youngest.

As they moved in line across the lake, Princess Lina's boat fell further and further behind.

"Why can it be?" she wondered. "We are not usually so slow."

"No," her prince answered. "Yet I am poling as hard as I can."

Still, they came to the castle at last and the prince led the youngest princess up to the great ballroom where her sisters were already dancing as though their lives depended on it. All through the night they danced, to a ghostly music that played unceasingly, while the air grew hot with the heat of a thousand candles whose light was reflected back in a dazzle of brilliance from the mirrors lining the walls. They danced until their shoes were worn into holes and then, when the first cock crowed, the music stopped and they all trooped out to the cool terrace where an exquisite supper awaited them. Michael too was hungry, but when he stretched out his hand to take a biscuit from a golden dish near by, he found that he held nothing but a withered leaf.

Last of all, before they prepared to return to their boats, each prince and princess raised a crystal goblet and drank a toast – to dancing.

On the way back, as they passed through the silver wood, Michael broke off a twig. It snapped with a clear sound like a bell and Princess Lina cried out,

"Oh! What was that noise?"

"It was nothing," said the eldest princess. "Only the hoot of an owl in the castle turret."

Before they reached the door, Michael managed to slip ahead and once back in the princesses' room he was out of the window and down the ivy in less time than it takes to tell.

When he made up the princesses' bouquets that day, Michael slipped the silver branch into the one for Princess Lina. She stared at it in alarm but said nothing to her sisters. Only, later in the day as she was walking in the garden, she came upon the gardener's boy and paused as if to speak to him then, altering her mind, went on her way.

When night came, Michael again put the flower of invisibility in his buttonhole and followed the princesses to the ball. This time, as they crossed the lake, it was the prince who complained that the boat seemed unusually heavy.

"It is the heat," Princess Lina said quickly. "I, too, am feeling very warm."

At the castle, all happened as before but, on the way back, Michael plucked a branch from the golden wood. It rang with a deep, mellow sound and this time it was the eldest princess who cried out.

"It is nothing," said Princess Lina, "only the boom of the bittern in the marshes."

That day, as she expected, Princess Lina found the golden twig in her bouquet. She resolved to speak to the gardener's boy.

"You know our secret?" she challenged him.

"Yes, Princess."

"I do not care how you know," she said, which was not true. "Only keep it close – or it will be the worse for you. Take this for your silence." And she tossed him a purse of gold.

"My silence is not for sale, Princess," said he, and left the purse where it lay.

That night Michael travelled in the boat of the eldest sister and although at the ball Princess Lina kept a sharp look out, she saw nothing to alarm her. Only, in the diamond wood, she heard one faint, high shriek.

"It is nothing," said her second sister. "Only the cry of a nightjar in the thicket."

But there, in the morning, was the diamond branch in Lina's bouquet.

Meanwhile her sisters had noticed the glances Lina cast at the gardener's boy and had seen her speaking to him.

"Are you going to marry him?" they asked her. "How delightful! To be a gardener's wife!"

At last their teasing made her so cross that she told her sisters what had happened. The other princesses were horrified.

"But he will tell our father!" the eldest cried.

"He hasn't yet," Lina pointed out.

"But how can we trust him?" they asked.

The youngest princess thought she knew. But she dared not say.

"There is only one thing for it," the eldest princess decided. "We must make him drink the magic cup that will make him one of us. Then he will stay in the enchanted castle and think of nothing but dancing for ever and ever."

The youngest princess looked unhappy but, as the others were all agreed, there was nothing she could do.

They sent for the gardener's boy and told him he was to go with them that night. Michael bowed silently, but he could not help one reproachful glance at the youngest princess and he thought he saw a tear in her eye.

Even though he knew they meant him harm, Michael was determined not to give away their secret, for the sake of the little princess. But, if he went to the ball, he would at least go looking like a prince.

He went to his laurel trees and said, "My beautiful rose laurel, with the golden rake I have raked you, with the golden can I have watered you, with the silken towel I have wiped you. Now dress me like a prince."

A beautiful pink flower blossomed on the laurel and, as he tucked it in his button-hole, Michael found himself clothed magnificently in black velvet with a diamond drop in his ear and silver buckles on his shoes.

In this princely attire, he went to the king and obtained leave to try and fathom the princesses' secret.

That night there was no need for invisibility. Michael entered the antechamber to the princesses' room as the other princes had done and waited until the door was locked and they were ready to start.

He gave his arm to the eldest princess, who was agreeably surprised by the appearance of the gardener's boy. When they reached the castle, he danced with each in turn, so gracefully that all were charmed with him. But most of all he danced with the youngest princess and those, he thought, were the happiest moments of his life.

Too soon the time came for them to drink their nightly toast. A page came and knelt before the gardener's boy. He held a golden goblet filled with wine.

"Now," said the eldest princess, "you have tasted the delights of the enchanted castle. Drink, and those delights shall be yours for ever."

He lifted his eyes and looked once at the youngest princess, then, quite steadily, he reached his hand to the cup.

"Don't drink!" the little princess cried, leaping to her feet. "I would rather marry a gardener!"

With that she burst into tears.

In one movement, Michael swept the contents of the cup to the floor and threw himself at Lina's feet. The other enchanted princes dashed their goblets to the ground likewise, for the spell that had held them all was broken.

Somehow, each princess found herself in a boat with the prince of her choice. Somehow, too, the remaining company passed by magic over the lake, while the enchanted castle crumbled quietly to dust behind them.

The king was still asleep when Michael and the princesses reached the royal bedchamber, but he had given orders that he was to be woken at once if anyone discovered the secret of the princesses' shoes, which Michael now revealed, producing the golden cup and the three twigs he had given to Princess Lina as proof of his story.

"Choose, then," said the king. "Which of my daughters shall be yours?"

"My choice was made long ago," was the answer and, as the youngest princess came to take his hand, Michael gazed deep into her velvet eyes and smiled.

The princess did not, of course, become a gardener's wife. Instead, the gardener's boy became a prince, a position he filled to admiration. He and Lina lived for many years in the greatest happiness and the two laurel trees long stood beside their door. Somehow or other, though, the golden rake and the watering-can and the silken towel appear to have been mislaid.